A BROKEN LINE

Table of Contents

PROLOGUE

It was her wedding day, a day that was supposed to overflow with joy and pleasure for Selma Raven, who'd wanted nothing more than to be united as one with her perfect half.

Yet, the young bride had found herself woken the night before her wedding to fumes and heavy smoke pouring in through the hallway.

Her house was on fire.

CHAPTER 1

Her name was Selma Raven, and she had it all.

Every morning Selma would wake up draped in the comfort of her parent's luxuries. She slept on a king-sized bed, wearing comfortable pyjamas that had been bought for the price of gold, in a king-sized room with every lavish item a person could desire.

Every item from her bedroom was an expensive rarity collected over time from various countries. Her father travelled a lot and brought a gift from every place he visited. Selma had a treasure from all 50 states in America in her room. They came in the form of dresses, furniture, jewellery, and even antiques that she kept around solely for the purpose of decoration.

There was no other room in the city of Landan like hers, but how could there be? After all, Selma Raven was the beloved and treasured only child of the wealthiest family in Landan. They owned properties in various other cities and had successful businesses all over the world.

With the amount of power and wealth her family had acquired, Selma had no reason not to wake up every day with a smile on her face.

She could have anything and everything she wanted.

However, that just was not enough.

There was nothing material Selma couldn't claim, from land to wealth. Everything that her father and mother owned was her by right. As an only child, that was never going to change. She'd gotten everything she'd wanted for her birthday and every holiday, but it still wasn't enough. She'd been spoiled silly.

Despite having everything, Selma found with a pang in her heart that there were certain things that money couldn't buy.

Due to their big and powerful name, her parents took every opportunity to protect their image, including banning her from ever getting involved with any of the children in their city. Selma was never allowed to play outside or frolic in the snow or the grass. She was denied having local friends and had all of her education completed abroad, away from the people who knew her name.

When she returned, she was a mystery to the people around her as much as they were a mystery to her. Rumours started flying when she returned to Landan, and nicknames arose as soon as people realised who she was. As the heir, of course, she took a position at her father's local co-operations. She was made the CEO in a second, and then everyone knew her name.

Selma Raven, the Diamond Princess of the Raven family.

Despite being qualified with the experience and the degrees to back her up, suddenly becoming CEO had further isolated her from the rest of her staff. They did their bidding and their jobs as she directed as they didn't want to lose their income, but they were cold.

Spoilt, pampered, and rich were the only things people saw when they looked at her. She was no better than the many co-operations her father ran.

In fact, they seemed to view her like she was yet another expensive jewel owned by the Raven family, and perhaps she was.

Then he entered her life. He changed everything.

"Good morning, sweetheart," Donovan whispered as he leaned over her to press his lips softly against her cheek.

Selma Raven fluttered open deep brown eyes, a smile slowly spreading on her lips as she woke to the view of her husband's handsome face before her.

Well, future husband, but time passed so quickly, and they were already engaged.

In under a week, they'd be married.

Just knowing that had Selma sitting up in bed, her heart lighting with joy. She pushed strands of her pale blond wavy hair out of her face so she could get a proper look at him. Donovan was the highlight of her waking up every morning.

"Might I interest you in breakfast?" Donovan teased. It was then she noticed the tray in his hands, and her smile widened considerably.

"What are we having?" she asked excitedly.

"What are we not," Donovan chuckled. "Sandwiches, bacon, eggs, toast, a little salad to the side with a cup of juice and a bottle of water."

As he spoke, he moved to tray onto her legs, sitting beside her as he waited eagerly for her reaction.

"I wasn't sure what you'd be in the mood for this morning, so I got you one of everything," Donovan admitted with a shy smile.

"Oh my gosh, Donny," Selma groaned as soon as the food passed through her lips. She slapped a hand over her mouth and looked at him in awe.

"It's bad, isn't it?" he asked in amusement.

"Ah, it's terrible," Selma giggled, and they both broke out in laughter.

"I really thought I'd finally broken through the Smith curse of bad food," he said dramatically with a shake of his head, and she giggled even more.

"Come on, it's not so bad," Selma grinned as she poked at the food. "See, the eggs are nice, and the sandwiches are......."

"Edible?" Donovan asked with a slight raise of his eyebrows, and she grinned.

"I was going to say..... salvageable," Selma chuckled, and he shifted even closer. So close that she could feel his warm breath on her cheek, and she leaned even closer to him in relief.

Donovan was not the best cook, yet he insisted on making her breakfast in bed every day. He hoped that one day he'd become good enough to make a feast fit for a Queen, a meal that she deserved.

He was her light, and she couldn't imagine what she'd do without him.

**

Selma had met Donovan in a bookstore.

As someone who could have every book she wanted to be delivered right to her doorstep, she had no reason to be in one, yet that day she'd walked in. Within books, Selma found peace as she could be anyone but Selma Raven. She could walk in another's shoes and live another's life. See things from a different point of view.

That day, she wanted to experience the joy of walking into a shop and finding something new. Knowing she could buy out the entire shop if she wanted, she limited herself with a rule that she could only pick out one book. Being able to only choose one made shopping harder.

Selma couldn't imagine living like all the poor people who couldn't afford what they wanted.

Finding a book that interested her, she reached out for it but accidentally knocked down the book beside it. With a huff of annoyance, Selma bent to pick it up and wondered how much she could pay someone to do it for her. However, before her hands touched the book, a larger set of hands lifted it from the floor.

"Don't worry, I've got it," the stranger said, and Selma froze as he raised his head.

Dark hair with deep eyes dark blue; the stranger was gorgeous. When he straightened himself, she also saw that he was tall. Lightly, he dusted the book before handing it back to her. Selma took in her hands, and he smiled politely. The next thing Selma noticed was the uniform. A police officer.

"Take care, ma'am," he nodded at her, tipping his hat before continuing down the aisle.

"Wait!" Selma called. She'd been speechless for a few minutes; that was unlike her.

She walked forward, strong, and confident, as she fished out some money from her purse and handed it to the confused young man.

"No, ma'am," he laughed. "You pay at the counter."

"I'm not paying for the book," she corrected. "I'm thanking you."

Selma had always made sure that everyone who helped her was duly paid.

Selma wished she could pretend, but she was no stranger to taking kindness. Co-workers would bring her drinks and presents in the hopes of financial favours. Even something as simple as this could be an officer of the Law fishing for some sponsorship. She knew how desperate those police hounds could get when it came to her father's money. They were basically Raven's lap dogs.

Besides, nothing was a coincidence when it came to her life.

However, to her surprise, the officer gave her a funny look.

"What?" she frowned. "Is it not enough?"

The audacity of him to silently ask for more. Not like she couldn't afford it, but if he wanted to beg, then he ought to beg for real.

The officer did not beg, nor did he ask for more. He just smiled, and there was a hint of sadness in the curl of his lips.

"I was told the reward for kindness would come in the afterlife," he said.

"What's the good in that?" Selma asked.

"You don't even know if you'll make it to the good side, so why not enjoy what you can right now."

"You have a point," he laughed, and Selma found his smile arresting. The easy-going drop of his shoulders, the way his eyes would close halfway when he smiled.

He was her type.

Selma ignored the thumping in her chest, only cocking her head curiously when he still turned her down.

"However," the officer said. "I'm not accepting pay for picking up a book. After all, I'd like to believe that there still are people in this world who are kind without expectation of reward."

He attempted to walk away with yet another smile, but Selma halted him again.

"Wait!" she cried, and he stopped.

"I don't know your name," she said, blushing as that was no novelty. She barely remembered her co-workers' names. They were all just the same people with the same need as her.

He felt different.

"Donovan Smith," he smiled. "You?"

His question shocked her.

Selma narrowed her eyes at him.

"Do you not know who I am?" she asked in suspicion, and he smiled.

"I have an idea," he admitted. "But it could be the wrong one. It's only polite to introduce yourself, don't you think?"

Selma smiled in amusement.

"My name is Selma."

The man turned away from her, facing forward, hands in his pockets as he seemed to consider her name. Then he turned back to her with a beaming smile on his face.

"That's a beautiful name," he said.

Selma ended up leaving the bookshop with no books that day. She didn't need any adventures or stories to sink into. She just might have found one of her own.

CHAPTER 2

Donovan Smith waited in the living room for Selma to come downstairs.

He was leaning against the table next to a little grouchy grey curled at the center of the beautiful furniture.

He'd had to get Selma something else to eat as his attempt at the bookshop, watched him with a dark glare.

Donovan had to admit that the name choice was ironic and cute.

Salem, Selma's exotic and expensive Persian cat. Everything in this house was expensive. Well, everything but him.

Donovan had started his life at an orphanage, packed in like sardines with a bunch of other kids.

No family, no friends, no rich family with an expensive name to benefit from. For most of his life, Donovan had been alone.

It hadn't been terrible at the orphanage, and it was just real. He'd grown up with many other children, and they'd loved each other like siblings. Like siblings, they'd had their own ups and downs, but they'd been there for each other, and when he'd become an adult, they'd encourage him as he became part and parcel of the police force.

Donovan had always been interested in crime movies and the sort. He didn't fancy himself a superhero and got apprehensive when it came to making certain decisions, but he never regretted joining the police, no matter how scary things got. After all, working such an obvious job had made it so much easier for Selma to find him.

"Hungry Salem?" Donovan asked, but the cat just glared at him. Salem was not really the friendly type, especially when it came to him. Donovan had researched a bunch of times how to win over your girlfriend's cat, but it just wasn't easy.

"Come on, don't look at me like that," he chuckled. "You're making me more nervous than I already am."

The wedding rehearsal was today.

After today, the next time he walked into a church would be to officially be one with Selma.

There was so much that came with marrying into the Ravens that Donovan was honestly worried about. He drummed his fingers on the table as he examined how he'd gotten this far.

Selma's father might not have accepted him had he not been a police officer. He'd proven himself bright and useful to Mr. Raven. He was intelligent and good at following orders. If he played his cards right, he would soon be up for a promotion. It was important to the Raven family that he got more control over the law enforcement of Laban. After all, it was important that the police remain the Raven family's loyal dogs.

"Honey, are you ready to go?" Selma called out, and Donovan straightened himself at once. He paused once again as he saw her coming down the stairs.

Selma was worth it. Every sacrifice he'd had to make, every difficult decision he'd had to swallow down. She was gorgeous as she came down the stairs in a long flowing white skirt. Her dress was strapless,

showing her pale shoulders, her hair falling down like white blond falls. As soon as they locked eyes, they stayed locked, her smile brightening as his smile widened.

Selma unlocked a soft part of Donovan's heart that he hadn't even realised he had. He wanted to give her the world, and he didn't know what to do about it as he'd never imagined that he would fall so fast or so hard. Selma had made him feel in a way that he hadn't felt in a long time. When he held her in his arms and kissed her neck till she giggled, he wanted to freeze time and remain in that moment forever. Sometimes the only thing Donovan feared was that tomorrow would come and rip Selma away from him. He was afraid that his family would decide he wasn't good enough. That the wedding would turn out to be fake.

Donovan couldn't help but laugh at himself at that last thought.

He'd proposed to the only heir to the Raven family. He should have known what he saw signing up for. It was something he would never let go of. His only hope was that Selma accepted him the way he accepted all of her.

He held out his hand and took hers in his.

"Donny," Selma smiled.

"I thought it was bad luck for the groom to see the bride in the wedding dress?" Donovan chuckled in amusement with a raised eyebrow.

"Don't worry about that," Selma grinned and gestured to the dress. "This is my 'wedding rehearsal' dress. You'll see the real dress on the wedding day."

Donovan sucked in a breath.

"You mean to tell me that this isn't even the actual dress, yet you look so gorgeous in it?" he breathed with love in his eyes, and she giggled.

"Hold unto your horse's future, Mr. Raven, because you're yet to see me at my best," she grinned, and he smiled.

Mr. Raven.

Yet another thing he would be giving up in this relationship is his last name. Something like that was supposed to mean nothing compared to being called part and parcel of the Raven family.

If he were to lose his whole identity, would Selma still love him? He was honest in his adoration for her, but he knew of the many scandals of the Raven family, as expected for a household that could buy anything they wanted, even concubines.

"Selma," he said as she wrapped her arms around his neck.

"Yes, darling?" she whispered into his ear, and he pulled her into a hug as close as he could without ruining her dress.

"I'm getting cold feet," he admitted, and she pulled away from him immediately, worried in her eyes.

"Donny, what's wrong?" she asked, and he detected a hint of fear in her voice. That was never his intention. He did not want to scare her.

"You don't want to marry me anymore?"

"No, baby," he said immediately and shook his head firmly. "I'm not scared of ever falling out of love with you. I'm scared that you might eventually be unhappy that you married me."

"That's nonsense. Why would I be unhappy?" Selma asked, confused, and Donovan smiled sadly.

"No one knows what tomorrow will bring," he said softly. However, Selma was unperturbed.

"Yet we agreed to make this vow to face it together no matter what," she said and wrapped her arms around him.

"Truly Selma?" he asked and leaned into her touch, her scent. "You won't let me go?

"Truly, Donny," she said with such surety in her voice that his heart ached. "I want to love you and only you."

Her words and hold were reassuring. When they raised their heads, they found nothing but love in the other's eyes. Together, they leaned forward, lips inches apart, when Salem suddenly lunged, much to their surprise.

Donovan fell back quickly so he wouldn't get scratched; Salem could get violent from time to time. Selma caught the yowling cat, but she was annoyed at their interrupted kiss.

"Oh, Salem behaves," she scolded him. "You'll ruin my dress!"

"Salem, careful," Donovan laughed, and he reached out to help, but Salem immediately charged at him, claws outstretched.

"Yowch!" Donovan gasped as those extended claws sunk into his arms.

"Salem, stop; you're going to ruin his clothes!" Selma gasped and once again snatched Salem before he could do any more damage.

Those claws were short, but they still hurt. Donovan winced while feeling very grateful he'd worn regular clothes instead of his quality outfit for the wedding rehearsal.

"No, no, it's fine. Don't blame the cat," he laughed.

"Oh, my gosh, Salem," Selma said, looking so disappointed in the little guy that Donovan chuckled.

"We're going to be late."

It was just one of those days, Donovan thought with a laugh, his hand rubbing painfully at his wounded hand while Selma scolded her cat.

Some people were cat people, and some people were dog people. They figured Salem didn't like him because he spent so much time around the police dogs.

"It's okay, Salem; you don't have to like me," Donovan smiled. Salem just jumped out of Selma's arms and walked off with his puffy tail in the air.

"He's eventually going to get used to you," Selma smiled. "Don't worry, I'll help you. After we get married, he'll just have to love you."

"After we get married," Donovan smiled and pressed his lips to Selma's hand. After they got married, the world would be a completely different place.

CHAPTER 3

The wedding rehearsal had gone as well as one could expect, though Selma would have preferred better. The rehearsal itself had gone perfectly, but everything that happened after left much to be desired.

"Are you really marrying a police officer?" some of her relatives whispered to her. "Or are you trying to surprise us by hiding the groom?"

Selma was shocked by the audacity they had to say to her.

They were having drinks and snacks prepared for relaxation after the rehearsal. She was looking forward to her approaching big day when some of her relatives decided to start a conversation while tossing dirty glances at Donovan, who was still trying to befriend Salem. He was cutely trying to woo her favourite kitty with some snacks. They'd brought him with them to the rehearsal, as even Salem had a role. He'd be her bridal cat, the first of its kind in Laban, as he was her oldest friend.

Everything had gone well, and Salem hadn't even attacked Donovan once during the rehearsal. However, here these people who claimed to be her family were ruining her good mood.

"Excuse me?" she frowned.

"I mean, he doesn't look like he has any personal wealth of his own," they continued, guests that her mother had invited. She didn't recognize them, nor did they impress her.

"What if he's just a gold digger."

"Who are you to judge my future husband?" Selma questioned with a warning in her time that made them back off.

"No, no, dear, don't get it wrong," they said quickly, their faces twisted in false concern. "You see, we're just worried about you. Our family has so many enemies, after all. Someone like him with a questionable background."

"An orphan at that, likely abandoned," another guest spoke up. "Why would his parents discard him if there wasn't anything wrong with him?"

"You-!"

Selma hadn't felt anger like this in a long time. That they dared say that to her, they dared slander her future husband and expected her not to react?!

She raised her hand in rage, and the guests panicked at the realisation of what she intended.

She was going to slap sense into them!

"Selma!" Donovan called and caught her hand before she could bring it down. Selma froze in surprise, and so did the guests. No one moved for a second.

Slowly, Donovan pulled down Selma's raised hand and brought it to his lips to kiss in adoration.

"My love, what's the matter?" Donovan said gently, and she slowly turned to look at him.

Her eyes were boiling with rage, but he was as calm as the still sea. He smiled at her with love, and her anger slowly washed away like sand at the beach. Donovan's silent message was received. These people did not deserve her anger or her reaction.

She let her hands go limp and calmed herself

"It's nothing," she said with a smile and turned away from those people without looking back.

"Come on, Donny, let's go."

**

"You know they have a point."

Selma couldn't believe the betrayal.

"Not you too, mum," Selma sulked, her eyes wide in hurt.

"I know better than anyone it's too late to object, but I wasn't so pleased with your choice," her mother admitted with a sigh.

When she'd brought Donovan home intending to marry him, her mother had not said much in protest. Selma got the feeling her mother thought she'd been joking. When she realised it was not a joke, her mother looked just a tad displeased but, once again, didn't dispute her decision.

When Selma shared what had happened at the rehearsal, her mother wasn't surprised.

"A man who works such a dangerous job," her mother tutted with concern. "Anything could happen."

"That's why we'll use our influence to make sure Donny never gets any of the difficult jobs," Selma said with a smile as she hugged her mother. "Dad is going to work on his promotion, you know. We're going to be fine, you'll see."

Her mother didn't look very convinced, but she did smile because Selma was smiling. They were the kind of family that delighted in each other's joys and stood by each other during times of trouble.

"Well, dear, as long as you're happy," her mother smiled.

Not long after that, her father returned home with Donovan and suggested a family dinner. The time she and Donovan could spend together as engaged was limited. However, her mother reminded him that they'd get every chance to sit at the table and eat together as one.

Pleased with this, Selma retired to her bedroom and waited for Donovan to join her.

**

"Can I come in?" he asked, peeking around the door.

She'd been waiting for him and threw herself in his arms, wrapping her arms around him and pulling him into a kiss.

"Selma," he whispered at her lips, and she pulled back when she noticed the tray in his hands.

"Whoops," she laughed and stepped back before she was upset about it. "Sorry, didn't see that."

"I missed you too," he said, and the love in his voice made her want to step forward and kiss him again. Yet Selma held back.

They settled together on her bed, and Selma grinned when she saw what was on the tray.

"Did you get takeout?" she laughed, amused.

"I didn't want to ruin tonight with my cooking," he said, and she giggled in amusement.

"Why didn't you just get something from the kitchen?" Selma asked curiously, and Donovan shook his head.

"I wanted us to have something special that was just us tonight," he said softly and pressed his forehead against hers.

"I hope you don't mind that I used your card. I couldn't find mine."

"Of course not," she said and nuzzled against him. Eventually, they moved closer, his arms wrapping around her as she sighed in bliss.

"After tomorrow, you'll be the new and improved Mr. Raven," she smiled. She turned to face him.

"Do you mind that? I know your name is all you have from whoever your parents were, but-"

"If I weren't fine with it, I wouldn't have proposed," Donovan said softly and stroked her cheek.

Relieved, she settled in his arms once again. They sat together, contemplating their future and dreaming of a brighter day ahead.

That day was never to come because Selma Raven woke to find her home ablaze on the night right before her wedding day.

CHAPTER 4

Selma rushed out, shocked to find everything she loved. The expensive furniture from all over the world, the exquisite art and rare jewellery, everything within the Raven villa was getting lapped up by the flames. The fire was spreading fast, eating up every part of the house. Everywhere but her bedroom, someone had gone out of their way to soak the floor a foot deep in water.

Scared and confused, Selma rushed outside and called for the servants. The villa was in a remote part of town so as to allow her family the privacy they deserved, but they had a large number of servants who all had emergency numbers on speed dials for situations like this.

What scared her the most was that Donovan had not been at her side when she woke up. Where had he gone?

"Father, Mother, Father, Mother, where are you?" Selma screamed as she ran through the halls. Nothing was moving in the villa beside her. It felt like a nightmare.

"Father-"!

"They're dead."

Selma froze at the familiar voice that interrupted her and immediately whipped around to find herself face-to-face with her dear future husband.

"Donovan," she gasped in relief and raced to him, throwing herself in his arms. "Donovan, thank God you're okay."

It was hard to fight back the tears in her eyes. Waking up to this nightmarish scene could send anyone into turmoil but Donovan being okay made her feel a little less alone. Donovan wrapped his arms around her and pulled her back into her bedroom, sealing the door behind them.

"We don't have much time, Selma," he said softly. "There's a rope cloth outside your window. If you climb out, you will find a suitcase in the woods. There's money in it. You should take it and-"

"Wait, wait, wait, what are you talking about?" Selma demanded. "What do you mean 'they're dead, who is dead?"

"Everyone," he replied with a gaze so cold that she had to take a few steps back.

She did not recognize this person.

"The fire," he continued. "Started in your parents' room."

"How do you know that?" Selma asked softly, and Donovan took a deep breath.

"Because I set it there, Selma," he said, but she shook her head in disbelief.

"You wouldn't do that," she said shakily, her lips trembling as she fell backward. "You...you can't. You won't. Donny. Why would you-"

"Because my name is not Donny."

He spoke with such calm that it left her feeling afraid and alone. He was unfazed by her tears and her fear; he spoke as he'd prepared for this outcome for a very long time.

"My real name is David Baker," Donovan Smith said as the lies began to fade away.

"And your parents killed my family."

CHAPTER 5

David will always remember the day the car came crashing into his life. It was, unfortunately, a scene that replayed countlessly in his mind. He'd thought of that moment, wondering if there was a chance that he could go back in time and fix what happened, but none of it had been anything he could control.

It hadn't been his fault, neither had it been theirs.

His father and mother had been seated in the front while he was strapped into the back playing with one toy or another. He'd been so fixated on it, like it was the most important thing in the world, ignoring his parent's argument about pies. His life had been that kind of life with a warm home, loving parents and simple moments like making a big deal about which pie was the pie king. He'd never expected that his whole world would get crushed so violently.

None of them had seen the car. They'd stopped at a traffic light as they should, but that car kept speeding like it owned the road. It slammed right into his father and mother.

David remembered briefly losing consciousness and the people who had fished him out of the car. He'd been disoriented and in pain. More pain than his little body had ever felt in his life. The accident happened in the middle of the afternoon in broad daylight! So many people had seen it happen. The car that hit them didn't even pause. It just drove off.

A few passer-bys had been kind enough to stop to help. They dragged their broken bodies out of the car, only then realising that his parents were long gone. Still, they did the best they could. The police were called, and all three were taken to the hospital. His mother had been pregnant. David had expected he'd go to the hospital to see her deliver his new baby sibling. He'd never expected death. That car had taken his whole life away.

David remembered, in and out of his memory, a man loudly declaring that they would get justice for his family. He'd taken a picture of the car's plate number. They would be reported to the police, and the bad guy would go to jail. Punishing the bad guys would not bring his family back, but it was the least the police could do. Every day he would ask the cops if the bad guys had been caught yet. Suppose they were not in jail.

The police took the investigation as seriously as they could at the time, and within record time, they'd found the car. However, as soon as they did, the entire case was dropped, and no one spoke a single word about it again. The visitors who had been showing up in the hospital encouraging him to get better and that the bad guys would get justice stopped showing up. Soon the police stopped showing up as well. He would repeatedly ask that the bad guys would be punished, but people stopped answering him. Eventually, someone even told him to move on. This was because the bad guys were the Raven family.

David hadn't understood at that time, but the Ravens were untouchable. When he eventually got shipped to the orphanage, he started his little investigation the best he could. He remembered the plate number the man showed him and traced it as best as he could. It was not easy for an eleven-year-old boy to work alone. When he finally found the car, it was crushed at the junkyard despite his cries and pleas for them to stop.

The junkyard owner threw him out even after he explained his story and told him he was better off dropping the case.

It was the same everywhere. Even after he grew up to join the police force, hoping to become a detective to find out who had killed his family, hoping the information would bring him peace. However, he hadn't been in the force long before he found out who. Everyone knew who got away with terrible crimes in Laban – the Raven Family. They could commit any and every crime known to men, from drugs to assault, to murder and not a hair on their pretty, rich heads would ever see the inside of a cell. The people of Laban who became their victims fell silent if they didn't want to be removed from the map. That's how dangerous the Raven family was.

With enough research, David found that the one driving that day had the Raven family's Patriarch, Selma's dad. However, knowing did nothing but create a desperate hole in his soul for a crime that would never get resolved. Clearly, he would never get justice by waiting for the law. The only way to truly get his vengeance was to infiltrate that family.

That was when Selma came home.

The plan had been to seduce her so he could get close enough to her criminal household. Falling in love had never been part of the plan.

**

"Donny," she said with pain in her eyes.

"David," he corrected once again.

The plan had been to frame her for the murder of her family.

It was easy.

"Everyone in this house was drugged, right down to the smallest servant," he said.

"How did you-?" she started in fear.

"The kitchen," he muttered.

It had been easy to contaminate every single thing inside of it. That was why he made sure she got used to eating only what he fed her.

"The entire staff and your family are deep in slumber. There is no point running or calling for help, and no one will save you."

Selma fell back on the floor, and David thought he could see her heart shatter.

"I'm not going to kill you," he said softly.

"You killed my entire family!" She screamed and threw a vase at him.

It was ironic.

David dodged the case and marched forward. Selma tried to scramble to her feet, but he grabbed her effortlessly.

"Would you rather I kill you too?!" he demanded. "Do you want to die, Selma Raven? Is that your wish?"

"Fuck you!" she cried as tears fell from her eyes. "Fuck you! You monster! I hope you burn in hell."

"And you said you'd always love me," he smiled in amusement.

"You expect me to matter when you do this?!" she demanded.

"Then imagine how I felt, Selma?" he ground out with bitterness and pain in his heart.

"I was a child. My mother was pregnant, and I was a child!"

She faltered but bitterness still burned in her eyes.

"You-" she cried. "I didn't do any of that to you."

"I know," he admitted.

Children were always the ones who suffered for their parent's crimes.

"That's why you don't die," he muttered, letting her go. She flopped to the floor again, her legs weak from the revelations. She felt sick, like throwing up, but all she did was cry.

"Your Raven family is good at concealing crimes, right?" he muttered. "Then cover up this one as well."

He didn't wait for her response before grabbing her. Selma screamed and kicked, but he grabbed her tight and held her out the window. In a panic, she tried to scramble back through, but he shook her firmly.

"Selma!" he yelled, and she snapped out of her panicked haze.

"The mansion is on fire, and you're going to die!" he yelled at her. "Do you understand me? You have to climb out of this window. There is money you can use outside so go!"

"Wh-what are you doing? Where are you going to go?" she asked shakily, and he smiled sadly.

"What do you care about? I thought you hated me," he chuckled.

"Donny, what the fuck are you doing?!" she demanded, seizing his arms in a vice grip.

"David," he corrected, and she took in a shaky breath.

"D-David," she said. The name felt foreign on her tongue like she called a stranger. He was a stranger, wasn't he?

"My parents are dead," he said softly, like he had nothing more to live for. Like he was sad and unfortunate, it infuriated her.

"My parents are dead!" she screamed back.

"It's different," he said firmly and refused to let her climb in through the window. The smoke had started infiltrating the room. The water wouldn't hold the heat of the flames back for long.

"You have money and power. You can stand on your feet."

"Don't you dare! Don't you dare pull that stunt with me," Selma screamed, her blond hair whipping in the wind. Her brown eyes were wide, and she looked almost like a fierce warrior.

"You got us into this mess! You got me into this mess," she cried. "You made me love you, you sick bastard."

She hated this feeling. It was one that she did not recognize. It was like watching her first pet hamster die and not knowing the reason. The death of everything she knew and loved.

"Don't do it," she begged him and hated that it had come to this. "Don't leave me on my own."

"Listen to what you're saying," he said, shaking her in disbelief. "I just murdered your parents."

"David Baker!" she snarled so fiercely that he fell silent.

"Do not leave me!" Selma commanded.

"If you feel that bad about killing my parents, then live the rest of your life as my property. Atone for your sins by giving me your life. Just don't you dare leave!"

David stared at her in awe, his vision partly fogged and watery in the smoke.

Yeah, that's what it was. The smoke and nothing else. It couldn't be anything else.

"You," he said, ignoring the choke in his voice. "You're really something else."

"I'm not leaving this mansion without you," she glared, and he chuckled softly.

"Well then," he said as the floor began to heat up.

"We don't have any time left."

There was no more time to spend talking. It was a big villa, but they had to outrun the fire.

David grabbed Selma and jumped out the window. He slid down the cloth rope that was dangerously heated by the flames. He and Selma managed to pass the floor without sustaining any injury. After that, they raced into the woods and didn't look back.

They ran fiercely in the direction where David had hidden the money, not stopping till David suddenly got attacked by a flying animal.

"Ow!" he cried out and hit the grass, surprising and scaring poor Selma.

"What was that? What was that?!" she demanded in fear. The animal approached her and leaped into her arms. Selma readied to throw it but paused in realisation.

"It's Salem," David groaned as he coughed out smoke.

A small weak part of him had been unable to bear the thought of making Selma part with her cat in such a violent way. The animal had hated him with good reason.

Selma wrapped her arms protectively around Salem and cooed at him, realising he'd been right all along.

"Oh baby, I should have listened to you," she said as she rocked him, and David smiled.

It had been so long since David Baker had felt so alive. His life had ended with his parents, giving way to the fake Donovan Smith, who had been completely consumed with revenge.

To bear his true name again, to have saved the love of his life. David had no idea what the future would bring but decided to take tomorrow one step at a time.

It was just him, her, and the stupid cat.

THE END

www.ingramcontent.com/pod-product-compliance
Lightning Source LLC
LaVergne TN
LVHW010510160826
845677LV00012B/2762